Products During
COVID
Chemical Engineering
Made Simple

For intended purposes, the illustrations have been simplified to understand the key purpose of the production process. It is by no means a comprehensive representation and/or replacement of the actual processes.

My Perseverance.

The year **2019** marked a historic moment for humanity as a deadly pandemic swept across the globe.

The coronavirus (or **COVID—19**) has indeed changed the world in which we live. What was once normal is no longer normal.

Purchases of everyday products skyrocketed with store shelves emptied overnight, leading to supplies becoming unavailable nationwide.

It was a sight to behold!

The role of chemical engineers became crucial in maintaining product quality control and producing supplies at a rapid speed.

Let's look at the products that became closely associated with COVID-19.

Face masks were mandatory, and a physical distance of 1.5 to 2 m was enforced between individuals in public areas to reduce the risk of viral infection.

These masks were made from synthetic, non—woven fabrics scientifically known as thermoplastic polymers.

Face Mask

1. MATERIALS

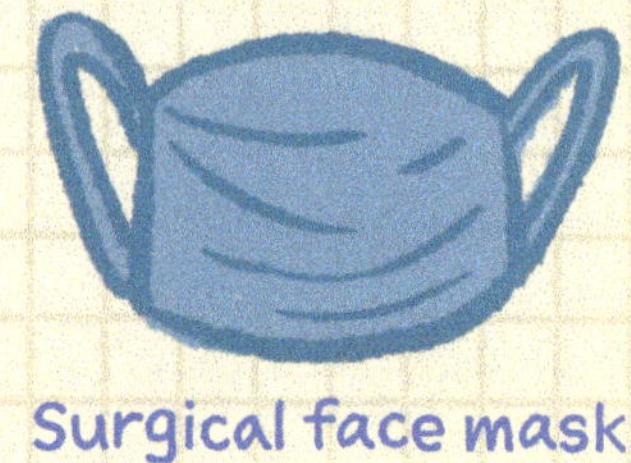

***Polymers:** have a repeated hydrocarbon backbone of hydrogen (H) and carbon (C).

****Melt blown technology:** the melted plastic is forced through small slit holes together with high temperature (230-360°C) air. The fast-moving air turns the plastic into tiny fibres.

2. PROCESS

Extrude

Web Formation

Bonding

3. PRODUCT

Surgical face mask

4. PROGRESSION

Variety

Wearing **gloves** was essential in high—risk sectors such as healthcare, hospitality, retail, and cosmetics to minimise close contact and protect against contamination.

Disposal gloves came in many colours including white, blue, green, and black, with each colour commonly used for a specific purpose.

Gloves

1. MATERIALS

2. PROCESS

*Vulcanization: a non-reversible chemical reaction carried out at an elevated temperature that causes polymer chains to crosslink.

**Chlorination: used to alter the grip properties of the outer surface of the glove to improve its performance.

Several **treatment tanks** are used in the process!

Coating tank

Beading
Cuff of glove is beaded to prevent tearing during donning (putting on) and doffing (taking off).

3. PRODUCT

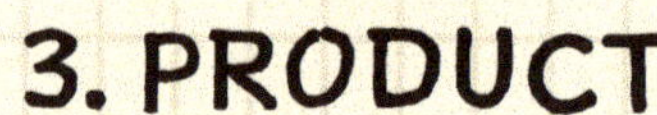

4. PROGRESSION

It was critical to carry an **alcohol—based hand sanitiser**
while travelling on public transport.
The alcohol helped kill bacteria and viruses.

As every organisation and family stocked up, hand sanitisers from
all brands became unavailable for months due to supply shortages as
manufacturers could not keep up with consumer demand.

Hand Sanitiser

1. MATERIALS

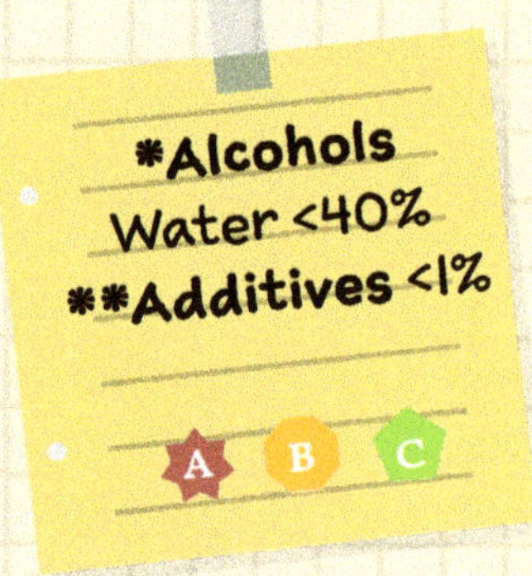

***Alcohols:** high concentrations (96%) of ethanol (CH_3CH_2OH) or isopropanol (CH_3CH_3OH) are used for their antibacterial properties.

****Additives:** other compounds are added to give the end−product its texture, colour and smell.

2. PROCESS

High Shear In−Line Mixer

*****In−Line Mixer**
Recirculates the mixture inside the tank to ensure uniformity of the product.

$$CH_3CH_2OH$$

Agitator

***In−Line Mixer

4. PROGRESSION

3. PRODUCT

COVID-19 drive-through testing sites were established to manage the testing process and provide results. Long stem **cotton buds** were used to swab the back of the throat and inside the nose.

People who tested positive were required to self- isolate at home for a 7-day period to monitor their symptoms.

Cotton Bud

1. MATERIALS

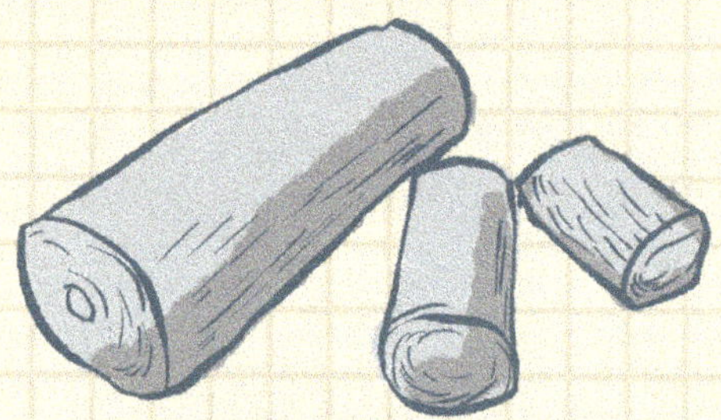

Pure cotton

2. PROCESS

Cotton cutting

Stick insertion

Gluing & **Drying

> ***Sticks:** different sticks types need different manufacturing machines. They can be made of paper, plastic or bamboo.
>
> ****Drying:** using a microwave oven to remove moisture and improve product quality.

***Sticks** (from hopper)

Single or **double** head cotton buds can be made!

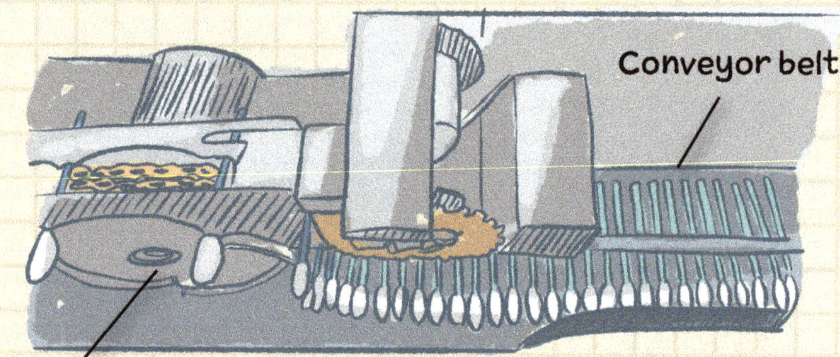

3. PRODUCT

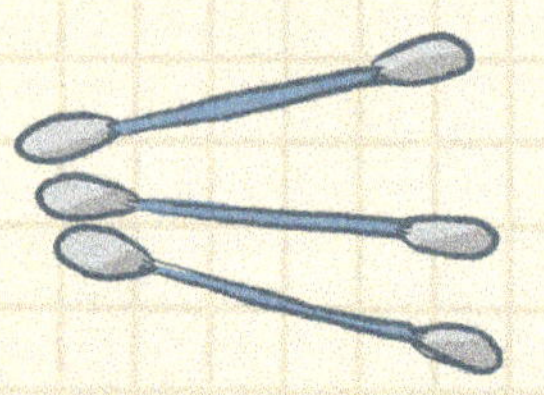

4. PROGRESSION

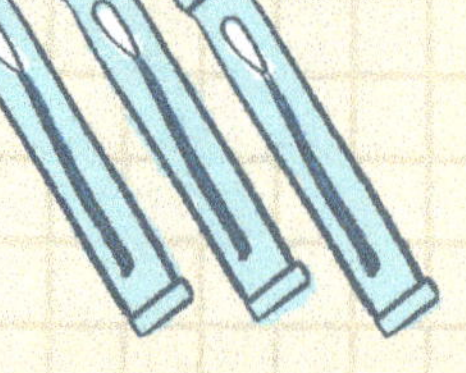

Bundle (domestic use)

Plastic seal (medical use)

It was a race against time to develop a **vaccine** to combat the virus. The world united as researchers, pharmaceutical companies, and governments worldwide pooled their resources and worked together.

Vaccine

1. MATERIALS

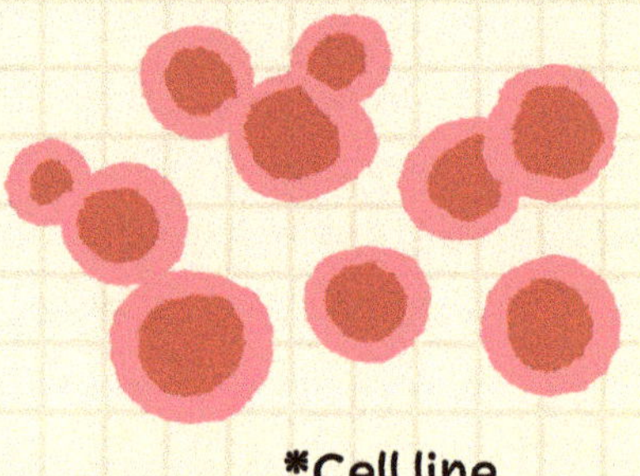

*Cell line

***Cell line:** a type of cell selected for amplification of the identified virus strain.

****Infection:** Grown cells at a certain cell count are infected with the virus strain at a desired quantity.

*****Bioreactor:** used for large-scale cultivation of cell types. The environment is regulated for optimum cell growth and product quality.

2. PROCESS

Cultivation

**Infection

Harvest

***Bioreactor

Temperature, pH, and oxygen concentration in the medium must be controlled!

3. PRODUCT

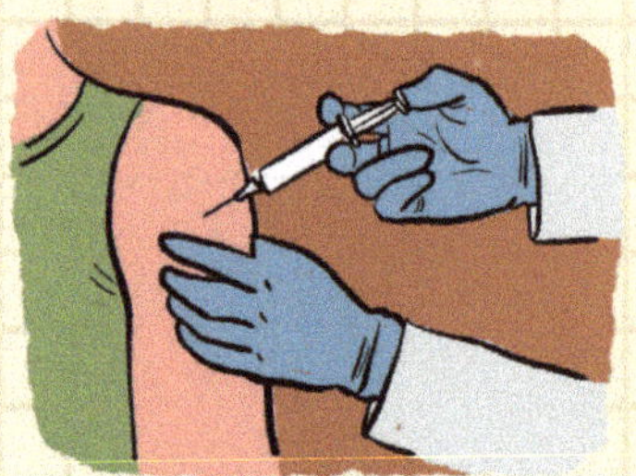

4. PROGRESSION

The vaccine was to stop people from becoming
seriously ill if they caught COVID-19 and was
administrated via a **syringe.**

Syringe (plastic barrel)

1. MATERIALS

*Polypropylene

Polypropylene (PP): has a chemical formula $(C_3H_6)_n$. It has a melting point of 160°C.

Injection Moulding: parts are produced by injecting molten material into a mould. Once the material cools down the plastic product is popped out.

2. PROCESS

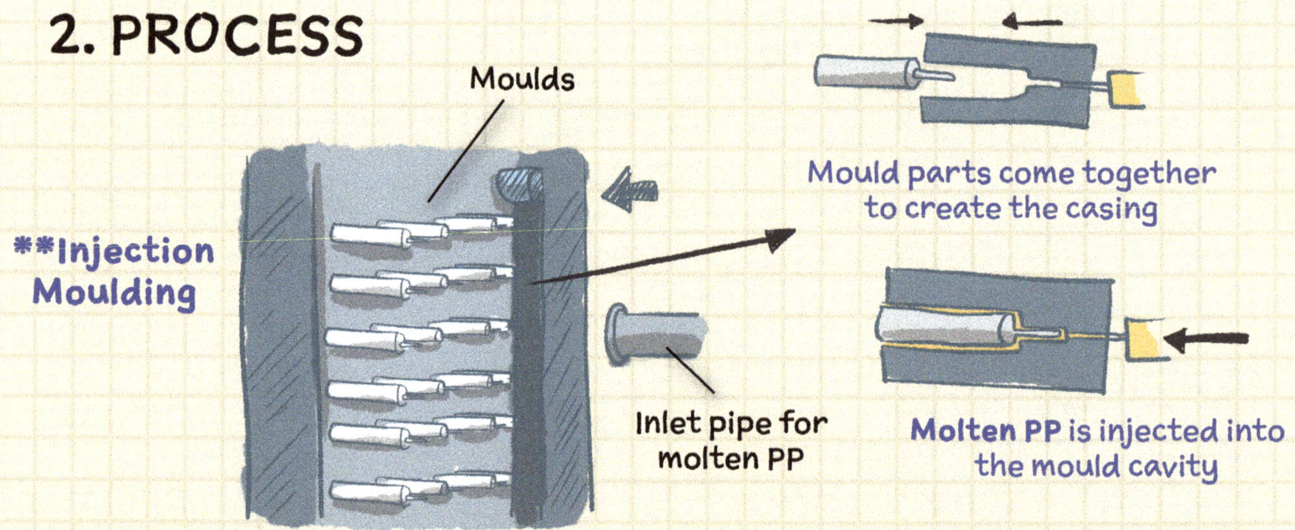

3. PRODUCT

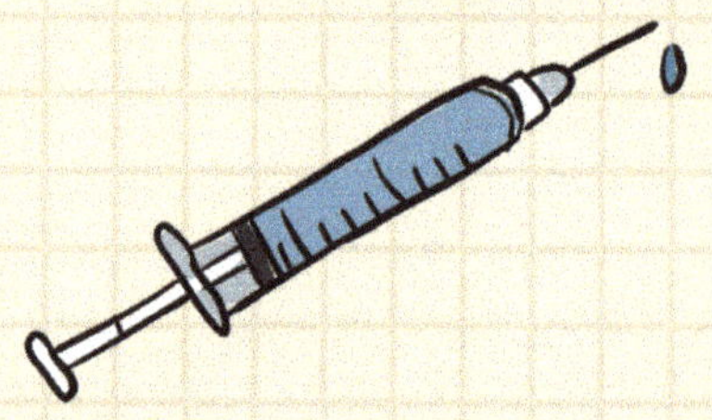

4. PROGRESSION

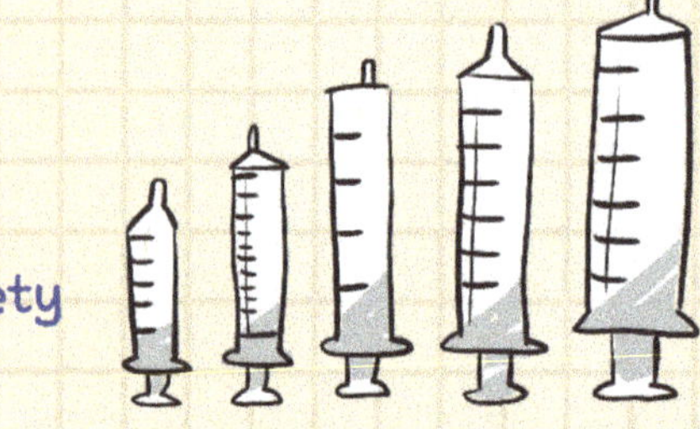

As more people tested positive for COVID—19, the lockdown triggered a surge in the use of electronic devices.

Working from home was necessary to control the pandemic while hospitals were understaffed and struggled with overcapacity.

Online meetings became crucial for maintaining communication and keeping industries operational. As a result, **computer screens** quickly sold out.

Computer Screen

1. MATERIALS

*Liquid-crystal display (LCD)
or
**Light-emitting diode (LED)

***LCD:** a layer of liquid crystals sandwiched between two transparent electrodes. When an electric voltage is applied the crystals align to control the amount of light passing through them.

****LED:** a type of semiconductor device that converts electricity into light.

2. PROCESS

Screen parts

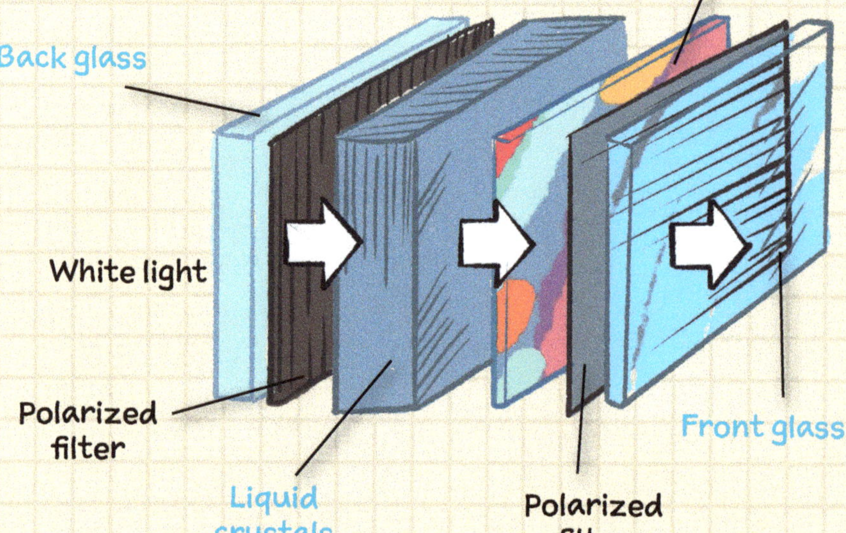

3. PRODUCT

4. PROGRESSION

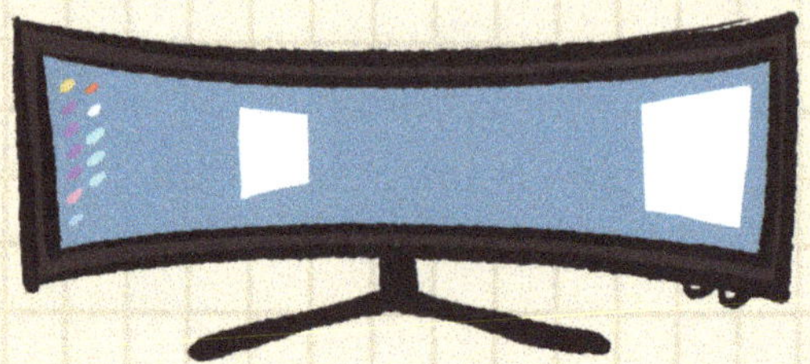

Curved screen

During lockdowns bread baking became a global trend as people were confined to their homes. Basic ingredients such as **flour** became highly sought after as many turned to making food from scratch.

Flour

1. MATERIALS

Wheat

2. PROCESS

*Conditioning

**Milling

Sifting

**Milling process

Including different **additives** such as vitamins, minerals, bleaching agent, oxidising agents, and salt, will change the end–product!

3. PRODUCT

4. PROGRESSION

Cake flour

Bread flour

Plain flour

Variety

Canned food was also recommended when
fresh produce was limited.

Tin Can

1. MATERIALS

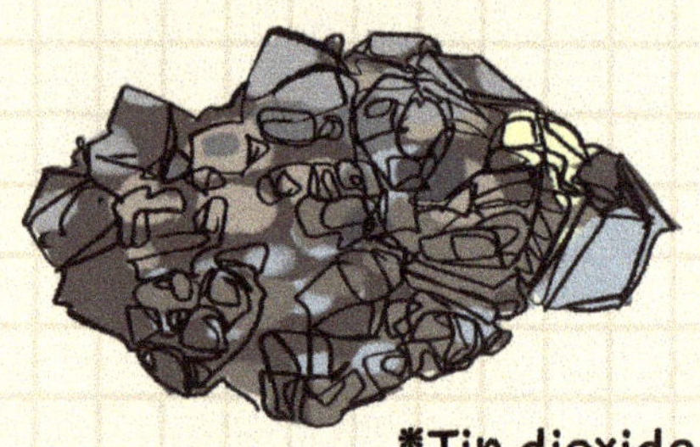

*Tin dioxide

2. PROCESS

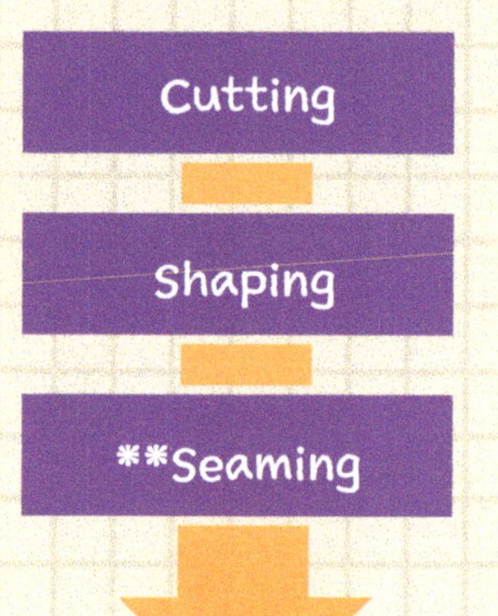

Cutting

Shaping

**Seaming

**Seaming process

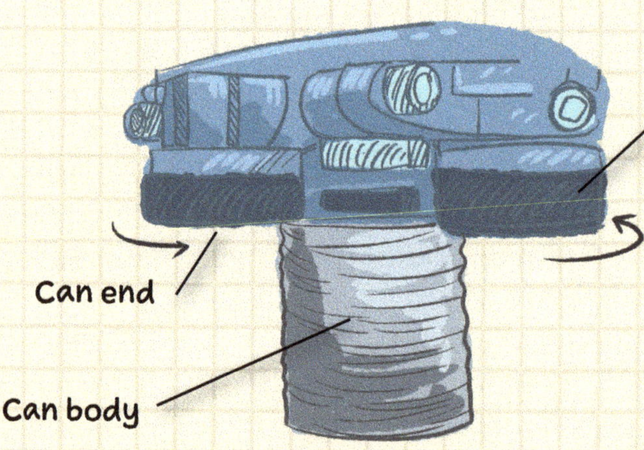

3. PRODUCT

4.PROGRESSION

Aluminium

Stainless steel

As we emerged from COVID—19, online shopping and
contactless purchases continued to
rise leading to an increase in **credit card** usage.

Handling and exchanging money were avoided to
prevent the spread of the virus.

Chemical engineers continue to work closely with doctors, medical specialists, and pharmaceutical companies to develop safe and effective vaccines for immunisation.

The Countries Best Prepared To Deal With A Pandemic
United States
United Kingdom
Netherlands
Australia
Canada
Thailand
Sweden
Denmark
South Korea
Finland

By promoting good health and hygiene we can prevent the spread of infections and illnesses, protecting ourselves and others.

COVID—19 is now a part of our lives, much like the flu. Remembering the importance of health, solidarity, and preparedness will help build a stronger and safer world.

The End

Also By Diana Tran

Process to Progress: Chemical Engineering Made Simple

Chemical Engineers Where Do We Work?

Chemical Engineers Where Do We Work? 2

Milk: Through the Eyes of a Chemical Engineer

9 780645 239881